PLANET DOOM

ANNE SCHRAFF

PAGETURNERS®

SUSPENSE
Boneyard
The Cold, Cold Shoulder
The Girl Who Had Everything
Hamlet's Trap
Roses Red as Blood

ADVENTURE
A Horse Called Courage
Planet Doom
The Terrible Orchid Sky
Up Rattler Mountain
Who Has Seen the Beast?

MYSTERY
The Hunter
Once Upon a Crime
Whatever Happened to
  Megan Marie?
When Sleeping Dogs Awaken
Where's Dudley?

DETECTIVE
The Case of the Bad Seed
The Case of the Cursed Chalet
The Case of the Dead Duck
The Case of the Wanted Man
The Case of the Watery Grave

SCIENCE FICTION
Bugged!
Escape from Earth
Flashback
Murray's Nightmare
Under Siege

SPY
A Deadly Game
An Eye for an Eye
I Spy, e-Spy
Scavenger Hunt
Tuesday Raven

SADDLEBACK
EDUCATIONAL PUBLISHING
www.sdlback.com

ISBN-13: 978-1-68021-379-9
ISBN-10: 1-68021-379-2
eBook: 978-1-63078-780-6

Printed in Malaysia

21 20 19 18 17   1 2 3 4 5

PAGETURNERS® | ADVENTURE

Chapter 1

Who would ever forget the night the amusement park burned down? Its grand opening had been one week away. Reggie Daniels and his girlfriend, Joanna Peck, had been high school students then.

Now it was more than two years later. They were both working and taking courses at City College.

Like everybody else, Reggie and Joanna had heard the sirens. They had seen the wild flames dancing hundreds of feet into the air. The smoke poured into the sky. It blotted out the moon and the stars. For a while neighbors feared that half the city would burn. But the fire department did a good job. They even saved many of the buildings within the park. But the park had never had its opening.

It was a Saturday night. Reggie and Joanna were on a date. The two stared at the ruins behind the ugly plywood walls. Big signs were plastered all over them. They read "No Admittance."

"Why don't they just tear the whole mess down? Then they can build something else here," Joanna said. The burned amusement park was now an awful eyesore in the neighborhood.

"Dad says they want to raze the place. Build a shopping center," Reggie said. "So far, though, nobody has enough cash. Everybody's offering pennies on the dollar for the land."

Five years ago, everything had been different. Eddie Scott, a kid from the neighborhood, had made it big in baseball. He was a star. An American League team had drafted him. The team had signed him to a multimillion-dollar contract. Eddie was one of the few from these mean streets to ever have such luck. He was so grateful.

He decided to help his neighborhood by building a state-of-the-art amusement park. He called it Planet Doom because it had an outer space theme. But then the fire had broken out. All his dreams had gone up in flames. Eddie's career soon flamed out too. After two years he was cut from the team. Then he vanished. Nobody knew what had happened to him. Worse, nobody cared.

♦ • ♦

Joanna peered through a narrow crack between two pieces of plywood. "It looks so weird in the moonlight. I can still see the Ferris wheel and the roller coaster. What fun we would have had if they'd gotten it up and running."

"My buddy Erik says there's a curse on the place," Reggie said. "That's why nothing worked out." Reggie laughed. Then he made spooky sounds, mimicking the ghost who maybe roamed through the deserted park.

Joanna poked him playfully in the ribs. "Oh, stop it! There's no curse. Some fool probably just tossed a cigarette into a pile of trash on a hot windy night. That's why it all went up in flames."

"I don't know," Reggie said. "I heard that some weird old dude owned this land a long time ago. They say his wife finally had enough of him and left. When she ran off, they say the old man put a curse on the house and the land. Then his house burned down. When they built the amusement park here, maybe the curse stuck."

"Oh, Reggie! Stop with the curse nonsense," she said.

"Eddie Scott must have been cursed too," Reggie said. "Say, what's with that dude these days? He gets millions of bucks to play in the majors. And he has one good season. Then he busts his ankle so bad. Nobody can fix it. He never did play great again. The poor dude must have been cursed. Or maybe the guy was just a jerk. Who knows?"

"Just some bad luck," Joanna said. "Happens to a lot of guys. The injury healed. But he lost his momentum or his confidence or something. Look at the stats. Plenty of guys who were Rookie of the Year ended up in the minors. They scrambled for less money than you get flipping burgers."

Joanna pushed at the plywood to widen the crack so she could see better. "I remember really looking forward to Planet Doom opening. It was going to be such a huge blast. At last we'd have something really fun to do in this crappy neighborhood. It seemed too good to be true. I guess it was."

Suddenly the plywood gave way. A two-foot-wide opening appeared in the fence. The space was plenty wide for somebody to slip through.

Joanna turned and grinned at Reggie. "It's only eight o'clock. I told Mom I'd be home by eleven. Want to take a look around?"

"Sure," Reggie said. "I always wanted to take a date to a haunted amusement park."

"Oh, Reggie, will you stop it!" Joanna laughed. "These are just some old deserted buildings."

When they had squeezed through the opening, Reggie carefully moved the plywood board back into place. He didn't want a passerby to notice the big opening and discover that someone had trespassed.

"Welcome to Planet Doom," Reggie said in a deep ominous voice. "Here you can travel to the farthest reaches of outer space. Are you ready to encounter terrors beyond your wildest nightmares? Abandon all hope, you who enter here!"

Chapter 2

Are you making that up?" Joanna asked.

"Nope. I'm reading it from that rickety old sign over there," Reggie said. "That's what it says."

"Oh," Joanna said. "Hey, you can still smell burned wood. Take a whiff," Joanna said. "And look! A lot of the park is still standing. It's a shame they don't do something about this."

"They *did* do something," Reggie said. "They fenced it off."

"I mean fix it," Joanna said. "Kids have nothing to do in this neighborhood. We've got one bowling alley. And there's a pizza parlor. There's nothing else but a lot of bars up and down this street."

"Yeah," Reggie said. "We don't even have a movie theater. We have to go to the mall to see the flicks. Maybe you and I should start a campaign to reopen Planet Doom," he went on.

"Oh, stop being a fool, Reggie," Joanna said.

Suddenly a voice called out. The public address system crackled. "*Welcome to Planet Doom. How nice to see visitors on a Saturday night. Even though we have not yet finished the renovations.*"

Joanna and Reggie almost jumped out of their skins.

"I'm getting out of here!" Reggie yelled. He spun around. Where was that loose board in the fence?

Joanna grabbed his arm. "You big baby! Some kid probably put that message on the PA system as a joke. You think we're the first kids who got in here? I bet plenty of kids have come in here to take a look around."

"I guess you're right," Reggie said. "But that voice really had me going for a minute. It was kind of funny, huh? Maybe we could leave a message for the next visitors. Let's see. 'Welcome to Planet Doom. Prepare to be eaten by a space octopus that is scampering toward your big toe right now!' "

"Yeah, right," Joanna said. "Look, there's a light burning in the old snack bar. I thought the electricity had been turned off long ago. Somebody must have rigged up a generator. Oh! And there's the hall of mirrors. Looks like it didn't burn at all."

"I bet all the mirrors are broken, though," Reggie said.

They stepped cautiously into the building. The two saw that the fire had blackened only one outside wall. Otherwise, everything seemed to be intact, even the mirrors.

"Listen," Reggie said. Then he read from a sign. " *You Earthlings are now entering the Venutian landscape. Notice that the planet rotates backward in a dense layer of clouds. Do you dare to open the mirrored door to Venus?"*

The mirrored door squeaked loudly as Joanna went inside.

Reggie followed. "Look up there," he said. "I bet that's the machine that makes the vapor. It would look like the cloud cover of Venus. It's so dark. I have to use my cell phone to see where to go. And even then it's confusing."

Joanna and Reggie walked down a hallway. They bumped into several false doors because of the mirrored walls. Suddenly the floor beneath their feet started rolling backward. Looking down, they saw that they had been walking on a moving sidewalk. Only it hadn't moved till now. It had begun to rapidly move backward!

"Whoa!" Reggie shouted. He stumbled and landed on all fours. Then Joanna lost her balance and fell too. "Shoot! I broke my phone," he cried.

"*On the planet Venus,*" a strange voice called out. "*There is a backward rotation. Perhaps you don't remember being told that in the beginning. Alas, it seems that you did not listen.*"

Joanna and Reggie finally got to their feet. They turned around, facing the direction in which the floor moved. Then a wheezing sound came from overhead. The room filled with white clouds. It was impossible to see.

"Man!" Reggie cried. "The vapor machine still works! This isn't funny anymore, Joanna! This is weird. We need to get out of here!"

The strange voice boomed out again. "*Ah, I suppose I should have told you. There is no life on Venus. The Venutian atmosphere is very hostile to all life forms. Especially to human life forms … human life forms … human life forms …*"

Chapter 3

I feel like I'm choking," Reggie said. He clutched his throat.

"It's your imagination, Reggie," Joanna said. "Come on, grab my hand. Let's go this way."

When they came into the next room, the thick vapor disappeared. They faced an entire wall painted in 3-D landscapes of Venus. The planet's rounded mountains seemed to stretch into infinity. Reggie and Joanna felt as if they could walk right into the desert-like terrain.

Then the strange deep voice filled the room again. *"In 1918 a great Nobel Prize-winning physicist, Svante Arrhenius, discovered that Venus had a hot, jungle atmosphere. Arrhenius said the planet was home to primeval monsters of the most awesome kind."*

Suddenly, across the landscape before them, strange and hideous creatures appeared. They were tall beings, covered in gray-green fur. Each of their swollen heads was dominated by one pulsating red eye.

"Reggie!" Joanna screamed. The creatures seemed to emerge from the wall. They came toward them.

"It's trick photography," Reggie said. "There has to be a movie projector behind us."

Then the normal lighting came back on. The voice said, *"We hope you have enjoyed your visit to the mysterious planet of Venus."*

"There's the exit!" Joanna yelled, running toward it.

The pair ran outside into the cool night air. The bright stars were above them. The sound of an airplane in the sky reminded them they were back in the real world.

"Wow, what a ride!" Reggie said. "It was really cool, huh?"

Joanna giggled. "Yeah, it was. And we didn't even have to pay for it. Dude, I was scared to death! That was just about the coolest thrill ride I ever took. What a shame they can't reopen the park for others to enjoy. It was so fun!"

"Yeah, now you say it was fun. But you were freaking out in there, Joanna," Reggie teased. "And my phone is broken. I can't even Snapchat this crazy place."

"My phone's battery is dead. I can't film either," Joanna said. "And you freaked out too! You imagined you were choking."

"I guess we can live without our phones. But I sure wish there was a vending machine around here," Reggie grumbled. "I'm starving."

"You ate almost half a pizza at the bowling alley," Joanna said.

"That was two hours ago, girl! I sure would like one of those big chocolate candy bars about now," Reggie said. "Is there anything in that machine over there?"

"Yeah, right," Joanna said. "This place burned two years ago, remember? The doughnuts in that machine would have turned to stone by now. The candy bars would be cement. One bite would break a tooth for sure!"

Reggie shrugged. He fished in his pocket for some change. "Wouldn't hurt just to look at the machine. Maybe the ghosts have a crew come in once in a while to stock it up."

The vending machine looked okay. Score! It had candy bars. There were little bags of nuts. And other snacks were still displayed behind small glass windows. Reggie stuffed in seventy-five cents. Then he pushed the button next to a chocolate bar. It dropped into the tray with a thud.

"The rock has landed!" Joanna laughed. "Look, a granite candy bar, yum-yum!" she said. "That must be so disgusting by now. It has to be petrified."

Reggie bit into the candy bar. "No, it's good. It tastes just great. Like the kind I get at the machines at my job." Reggie worked as a mechanic's helper at a car dealership. At night he took classes in automotive repair and computers.

"You're kidding me!" Joanna cried. "You mean they really last that long?"

Reggie broke off a piece of the candy bar. He offered it to Joanna. "Here, try it."

"No way! I know what a human garbage disposal you are. Even rotten stuff tastes good to you, Reggie," she teased.

They moved on toward a ride that took

passengers up in a little plane. The flames had burned off one wing. Now the lopsided wreck sat amid a tall pile of rubble. Reggie drew closer to the plane. "Hey, that's the kind of plane my grandpa piloted," he said. "I've seen pictures."

"Too bad it burned in the fire," Joanna said.

"Look!" Reggie yelled. "I just saw a guy up there in the cockpit!"

"Oh, come on, Reggie. It was just a shadow," Joanna said.

"No, I'm sure I saw someone. It was an older guy," Reggie insisted.

"Maybe they put a dummy in the plane, like they do at the car museum." Joanna craned her neck. "I don't see any guy in the plane, Reggie."

"Well, I sure thought I saw him," he said. But he now seemed much less certain.

"Oh, there's the little museum dedicated

to Eddie Scott," Joanna said. "It's blackened on the outside. It still might be okay on the inside. Let's go have a look."

They entered the museum. The sound system clicked on.

"*Welcome to the new Eddie Scott Memorabilia Museum. This exhibit is dedicated in gratitude to a fine young man from this neighborhood. His baseball career has made Planet Doom possible for the enjoyment of all, especially young people.*"

"Look! Here are pictures of Eddie when he was in Little League," Joanna said. "I was a kid when he graduated from high school. He was a real big shot to all of us. He took our high school to the championship."

"How old do you think Eddie Scott is now?" Reggie asked.

"Well, he got that big contract when he was your age, Reggie. I'm guessing he must be about twenty-five," she said. "I remember an article about him right after the park burned. The headline really stuck in my mind. It read '*Amusement Park Dream, Like Scott's Career, Goes Up in Flames.*' "

"Wow, it must have really hurt him to read a headline like that," Reggie said.

"I guess," Joanna said. They walked away from the museum. "Hey, look! There's the Mars ride. I wonder if that's as much fun as the Venus ride was."

"Well, the price is still right," Reggie said. "Come on. Be my guest."

Joanna and Reggie opened the door to the Mars ride. They saw it was a brilliant red inside.

"Hey, these little red cars look like real rocket ships," Reggie said. "Let's get in one of them and see where it goes!"

Chapter 4

Joanna glanced at her watch. "It's only a quarter to nine. We've got plenty of time. Yeah, let's do it!"

They each climbed into a car. The instructions said to tighten the straps over their laps. So they did. Joanna was in the car right behind Reggie.

"*Welcome to the Martian world,*" the deep voice said over the PA. "*Mars is very much like Earth. More than a hundred years ago it was said that a drought was threatening all life on Mars. The Martians sent pleas for help to Earth. Unfortunately, however, the Earthlings did not respond.*"

The cars moved down a hallway. The walls were painted to look like a Martian landscape. The scenes looked lifeless. Then they came into a great circular room. Giant 3-D pictures of Martian landscapes appeared all around them.

"There's a robot!" Reggie shouted. He pointed to a human-sized robot. It was clad in a silvery spacesuit. The robot had a huge bubble head. But its facial features were strangely unclear.

"Reggie!" Joanna cried. "It really is a robot. And it's coming toward us!"

He laughed a hollow laugh. "Hey, cool! A real robot. Hi, robot, what's your name?"

"My name is X7," the robot said in a metallic monotone. "I am a Mars expedition robot."

"Wow!" Joanna gasped in surprise. "I didn't think it would still work."

"Yeah. This place is full of surprises. I wonder what else it can do. Hey, stupid robot, what does this ride do? So far it's pretty boring. The Venus ride was a lot better."

Immediately there was a roar of engines. Next came the sound of gears. Then the cars whirled into motion. The cars began spinning around the room. At first it was exciting. But the little cars kept going faster and faster. Joanna and Reggie were dizzy.

"Stop!" Joanna screamed. She felt for an emergency button. The ride needed to stop now. "Boy, am I getting sick! I'm so dizzy I could barf!"

Suddenly the cars began to slow. With a jolt they stopped. The robot rolled close to their cars. It spoke to them. "I have four questions, Earthlings. Give the right answers. Then you will win a lifetime pass to Planet Doom."

"Stupid robot, we don't want a lifetime pass. We just want out of here," Reggie yelled. He yanked at the seat belts. But he realized that the belts were locked. Reggie couldn't get out of the car!

"Question number 1," said the robot. "Are you a baseball fan?"

"Yeah," Reggie said. "So what?"

"Your answer has been recorded. Question number 2. Do you know who Eddie Scott is?"

"Yeah! He's the dork who paid for this stupid park," Reggie snapped. "Let us out."

"Your answer has been recorded. Question number 3. Do you think it was fair for Eddie Scott to be cut after only two seasons?" asked the robot.

"Sure," Reggie said. "The guy was a total loser."

"Your answer has been recorded. Question number 4. Should Eddie Scott get another chance in the majors?" the robot asked.

Reggie laughed out loud. "I wouldn't let him play for my Little League club. Everyone remembers his final games. He sucked!"

"Your answers are not correct," the robot

said flatly. "You have not won a lifetime pass to Planet Doom. Instead, you will soon be departing. The subterranean ride is next."

"Hey, maybe that's cool," Reggie said hopefully.

Reggie's car zoomed ahead on the track.

"How about me?" Joanna cried. "Don't I get to come too?" But Joanna's car remained in place.

Reggie hadn't gone ten feet before he was drenched in water. In a few seconds the water came up to his chest. "Hey!" he screamed. "You can't do this to me! It's illegal to have dangerous rides. I am almost drowning!" Who was he yelling at? He didn't know. But he was mad. The ride's designer had to be crazy. This was not fun.

"Reggie! Are you all right?" Joanna screamed after him. "What's going on down there?"

"I'm soaking wet. The water is slimy. I want to get out!" Reggie yelled. "Yuck! It looks like swamp water. It smells like swamp water too!"

Then the deep voice rang out. "*You are now on Mars as it might have been eons ago. This was a time when Mars had water. There were many forms of microscopic life then. Perhaps there were insects too. Soon you will encounter some. Great diving beetles. Water lice. Water scorpions. And even small snakes.*"

"Help!" Reggie shrieked. "Get me out of here. Now the water's full of creepy stuff!" Dozens of creatures attacked him. But suddenly the car zoomed up the ramp. It returned to the room where Joanna was waiting.

Reggie waved his arms wildly. He knocked small creatures out of his hair and clothing. "Wait till I get out of here! I'm telling everybody what's going on in this horrible place," he said.

The robot slid over toward Joanna. It

asked her the same question it had first asked Reggie. "Question number 1. Are you a baseball fan?"

"No!" Joanna cried. She had no intention of going where Reggie had gone. No encounters with diving beetles and water lice! Ew!

Suddenly the seat belts in both cars disconnected. Joanna and Reggie leaped out. They turned back the way they had come.

"Let's find the quickest way out to the street," Reggie said.

"Yes," Joanna said. "I think it's this way. We'll try to backtrack the way we came."

"Man, I had no idea those dangerous rides still worked," Reggie said. The pair raced toward the fence. "I can't figure it out. Just wait till we tell the cops. This place is scary! I could have drowned down there! The cops will get on this fast. This park is a real hazard."

"Reggie," Joanna gasped. "There's still some horrible bug on your back. Gross! That one is hideous. It's got a million legs!"

"Get it off me!" Reggie squealed.

Joanna picked up a stick. She knocked the bug off.

Joining hands, the two sprinted ahead in the darkness. Then they heard the loud clanking noise of turning wheels. Joanna looked back. "Oh no! The robot is coming after us!" she cried.

"No way!" Reggie yelled. Joanna noticed there was real fear in Reggie's voice now. "Let's get going, Joanna. We can't let it catch us!"

Chapter 5

In a minute Reggie and Joanna passed the burned-out old plane ride. They had only about five-hundred yards to reach the fence. But now the robot had a weapon. It fired! A greasy gel spewed out. It covered the concrete pathway. The slippery surface forced the pair to slow down. The robot gained on them.

"He's right on top of us. We got to hide somewhere!" Reggie said.

There was a sign on the building just ahead. It said "Jovian Jump." Joanna pointed to it. "That way, Reggie. We'll hide in the Jovian Jump!"

Joanna and Reggie turned sharply. They slipped and stumbled on the greasy gel. Finally they scrambled into the large building. It was designed to look like Jupiter. There was a large red spot painted on the side.

Reggie and Joanna peered out a window. Had the robot spotted them coming in here?

"I don't see the robot anywhere," Reggie said. "After all, it's just a high-tech toy. It's programmed to do amazing things. But it can't think. It probably just kept going down the main walkway."

"I'm not so sure, Reggie," Joanna said. "There's something different about that robot. Like it's almost human!"

"You think?" Reggie asked nervously. "Like maybe it's not a robot? Maybe it's some kind of ghost."

"It could be a guy dressed up to look like a robot. Maybe it only looks like it's moving on wheels. Maybe there's a guy on skates. Or maybe it is something from outer space," Joanna said.

"Come on!" Reggie said. "That's too weird. Hey, let's see if there's a back door in this building. Maybe it leads to the street. I just want to get back to reality!"

"You said it," Joanna agreed. She grabbed on to Reggie's arm. Her fingers gripped so tightly that they tingled. "I can't wait to tell everyone what's going on. This isn't just some harmless ruin. It's really a dangerous place!"

"Too bad I broke my phone! This would be all over. We just need to get out of here," Reggie said.

"You know it! Lesson learned. Never leave home without a full charge," Joanna said. "Let's get going!"

"Look, there's a door. Maybe it leads outside," Reggie said. "We just need to get back to the fence. We don't have to go out the way we came in. I'll kick down a board. We just need to get to it."

Joanna opened the door. She peeked out into the darkness. There was no sign of the robot. "I think we're in the clear," she said. "Let's run for the fence. I don't want to spend another minute here."

They ran down the dark walkway toward the distant fence. Suddenly an odd-looking figure loomed in their path. Wearing a ten-gallon hat, it looked like a cowboy. The cowboy had a lasso. A plastic mask covered the cowboy's face.

"Howdy, kids," he called out. "You leaving Planet Doom already? Why are you in such a rush? I bet you haven't seen half of the park. Are you tired already?"

Joanna and Reggie exchanged nervous looks. "Uh, my mom expects me home by eleven," Joanna said politely. Was the cowboy just a crazy man? Why was he here?

"Yeah," Reggie said. "We need to get home, dude. No time for chitchat."

"Don't call me that," the cowboy said sternly. "Take the time to be polite."

"Sorry if I offended you, sir," Reggie said. "Um … we got to be getting home, okay?"

"You don't look like kids," the cowboy said. "Why leave now? Stay for a while. Have some fun."

"Who are you?" Reggie asked. "This place has been closed for years. Where did you come from?"

"I'm from the Lazy X27 Corral," said the cowboy.

This guy really was crazy. A cold chill went up Joanna's spine. She forced a smile to her lips. "Well, it's nice to have met you, sir. We appreciate your invitation to stay. We wish we could. But we really have to get home," she said.

"You been over to the Big League exhibit?" the cowboy asked. "It's the best thing in the park. Don't leave Planet Doom before taking a walk through it."

"Next time. We'll go there first," Reggie promised. He turned to Joanna. "Take my hand," he whispered. "We'll make a break for it. The fence can't be more than thirty yards away." Joanna nodded. Then the two of them joined hands. They broke into a desperate run for the fence.

Suddenly Reggie fell. The cowboy's rope had snagged his ankle.

"Hey, man, that's not funny!" Reggie yelled. Leaning forward, he tried to get the rope off. But every time he loosened it, the cowboy yanked harder. Reggie was dragged backward a few feet.

Joanna knelt. Working quickly, she loosened the rope. Reggie was free! He quickly scrambled to his feet.

But then the cowboy blew a whistle. Instantly, two huge dogs appeared.

"We're going over to the Big League exhibit now," the cowboy said. "You don't want these puppies to drag you over there, do you? They may dislike you. If they do, they'll chew you up and spit you out along the way."

Reggie and Joanna tried to make a move. But the dogs circled, growling and snarling. Foamy white saliva dripped from their jaws.

"We just want to go home," Joanna pleaded. "We never did anything to you. Can't you just let us go home?"

"Well, you can't always get what you want," the cowboy said. "Listen up. You'll get a kick out of the Big League exhibit. It's the experience of a lifetime. You don't want to miss it."

◆ ◆ ◆

Inside the exhibit was a small playing field. Stadium seats ringed it. The exhibit looked like a mini-ballpark! There were colorful ads like you would see in a real stadium. But these big signs were old and faded. Maybe this place was used to teach kids how to play baseball.

The cowboy seated himself in the bleachers. He sat near the big scoreboard. The dogs sat next to him.

"Play ball!" he shouted. He tossed a baseball to Reggie.

Joanna stared at her boyfriend. He stared back helplessly. The two nervously began tossing the ball back and forth. It was a game of catch. Then Joanna missed a catch. The cowboy hooted. Next Reggie missed one.

"Lousy little punk!" the cowboy yelled. "You're a loser. Nothing but a butterfingers. Throw the bum out! Send him back to the Minors!"

Finally the couple stopped playing. They'd had enough. Reggie looked up at the cowboy. "Okay, sir, you've had your fun. How about it? Can we go now?" he asked.

"Sure, get out of here!" the cowboy said. He held the collars of his two dogs. "Use the back entrance. Now go! And good riddance to both of you!"

There was an exit door. The frightened teenagers ran. Reggie pushed and the door swung wide. At last they were escaping!

Chapter 6

Reggie and Joanna slipped down a steep hillside. Where was the fence? The pair came to rest in a deep pit.

The cowboy's grinning face appeared above them. "Uh-oh! Guess I forgot to tell you about the ice hole. It's another fun ride. It was supposed to have water and frozen icicles. But the fire messed up the system. There used to be a ladder running up the other side. That was so people could climb out. But the ladder got lost somehow."

"Just throw us a rope, dude," Reggie yelled.

"Now don't get all mad," the cowboy said. "Why are you in such a hurry? Come on! You kids had some fun here tonight, right? This amusement park was built for kids like you. It was supposed to help the whole neighborhood. Tell me, did you have fun here?"

Reggie knew what the cowboy wanted to hear. Maybe he should try getting on the fool's good side. Maybe the man would toss them a rope. They needed to get out of the pit. "Oh yeah," Reggie said. "We had a lot of fun. This is a cool place. And we're coming back soon."

"This is the best amusement park. Ever!" Joanna added. "We'll come back every chance we get."

"Want to know something? The city plans to tear all this down," the cowboy said. "They want to build a shopping mall here. Can you imagine it? What fun is that? I thought they'd rebuild this park. But nope. What a waste." The man's voice had been sad. Now it hardened with anger. "They're even going to tear down Eddie Scott's museum. Can you believe it? They're going to erase his memory. He only tried to give some fun to the kids of his neighborhood."

"Uh, that's too bad," Reggie said.

"Liar!" the cowboy screamed. "You didn't think much of Eddie. I know you didn't. You probably screamed at him when he had a bad year. He was trying to live up to his promise. But nobody gave him a chance."

"Look, I hardly know who he was," Reggie lied. The truth was the opposite. Reggie and his dad had seen Eddie's last game. They watched as the baseball player had struck out. They jeered him.

"You called him a loser," the cowboy hissed. "Don't think I forgot about that."

Reggie recognized that voice now. He looked at Joanna in horror. The cowboy and the robot? They were one and the same! Whoever had been hiding in the robot suit was now hiding behind the cowboy mask.

"I didn't mean that," Reggie said desperately. "I was only joking. I was proud of Eddie for making it big. Hey, we all were. One of us getting the big bucks."

"Yes," Joanna added. "Eddie could have taken his money. Spent it all on himself. But he built this park for the neighborhood instead. He was a great guy. He was out to help us. Man, he was the best."

"You say that now," the cowboy said bitterly. "But none of you would give him a break. Not when he started to slip. Everybody loves a winner. But losers? They haven't got a friend in the world. All the fans turned on him. Eddie always gave his autograph to anybody who asked. But that all changed. People stopped asking."

"Did you know him well?" Reggie asked politely. He tried to make nice. Maybe the crazy man would throw down a rope.

"Sure did. Went to all his games. He was always nice to me. I played baseball too.

Never was a player like Eddie, though. Just played in the minors. But Eddie was real good to me. That's why I hang around here. Out of respect for him. I keep the generator going. Keep the vending machines stocked. I keep hoping people will come. Visit the museum. See his trophies. Appreciate the kid a little bit," the cowboy said.

Reggie felt bad for the sad man. "That's wonderful," he said. "It's really great that you're doing that."

"You're not the first to come through. No, not hardly. But the others were fans of Eddie's. They said nice things about him. They went on some of the rides. Then I gave them souvenirs. I could tell they liked that," the cowboy said.

"That would be cool," Reggie said. "To have something of Eddie's. Maybe you can toss us a rope. Then you can find a little memento of Eddie for us too."

The cowboy laughed. "Oh, it's a little

late for that. You already made your feelings clear."

"Oh no, sir. I told you I was only joking. Eddie was a great guy," Reggie said.

There was silence. "No! Once you get out of here," the cowboy said. "You'll call the cops. You'll whine. Complain about your bad time here. You'll report my dogs. Then the police will come. Reporters will swarm. They'll want to take pictures of me. The crazy old man who's kept this park alive. They'll write about that loser Eddie Scott. That's how the story will go. Then they'll tear down this place. Toss me into some hospital. Nobody will be left to remember Eddie. Nobody!"

"Hey, we'll keep quiet," Reggie said. "We promise."

"Yes! Just toss us a rope. We'll leave, honest! None of this ever happened. We won't say anything," Joanna said.

The man groaned. "Reporters are vicious. They tore Eddie to shreds. Made him look like a fool. Then Eddie got cut from the team. He couldn't get a job. Not even in the minors," the cowboy said.

"I'm really sorry," Reggie said. "But we didn't do it. We're just kids. And we need to go home now. But we're stuck in this pit. The walls are slippery. Please don't leave us here, sir. We'll die!"

Chapter 7

Well, I'm not going to kill you. I don't even have a weapon," the cowboy said. "I'm afraid of guns. The only defense I have are my dogs. You want to know their names? The brown one is Homerun. The black one is Shutout. They're real good dogs. They'll do anything in the world for me. Bad things happen. But it's not my fault. I'm a good guy. I don't even kill spiders. I take them outside.

"No one could blame me if you kids fell into this pit and couldn't get out. People would say it was just another accident. Like when Eddie broke his ankle. That's when he headed down the road to ruin. Accidents happen."

The cowboy sadly shook his head. Then he turned away.

"You can't leave us down here!" Reggie screamed. "It might be days before anyone comes by here! Or even weeks! You got to throw us a rope."

Reggie and Joanna could hear the cowboy whistling. The dogs yelped happily. But the sounds grew fainter and fainter. Pretty soon the only sound they could hear was the roar of a jet engine in the sky.

"Reggie," Joanna cried. "What are we going to do?"

"I don't know! How should I know? Maybe we could try crawling up again. But it's just too steep. We'd start falling back. The walls are so slippery!"

"But, Reggie, what if nobody comes? What if we're stuck down here forever?" Joanna asked. Her voice was thick with fear.

"I don't know why we came to this stupid

place anyway!" Reggie said bitterly. "The signs said not to. Why didn't we just walk on by?" His eyes narrowed then. "You were the one who touched the loose board. You said we should sneak in."

"You wanted to have a look as much as I did," Joanna cried. "If you didn't want to do it, we wouldn't have. Admit it! You wanted to come in too."

"Ugh. I know," Reggie said. "I'm sorry, Joanna. But how could we have been so stupid? My phone is trashed. Yours has no battery. And that dude is crazy! He is like a spider. And we are caught in his web like flies. Oh man! If only we'd gone somewhere else tonight. Then we'd be home in our beds sleeping now. And tomorrow we'd wake up and have a nice breakfast. Speaking of food, I'm starving!"

"You're thinking about food?" Joanna said. "At a time like this?"

"Joanna, don't you get it? We're doomed!

Why shouldn't I be thinking of my last meal?" he asked.

"Stop talking like that! By now our parents know something is wrong. We aren't answering our texts or calls. I'm sure they're looking for us. Before long, they'll call the police. They'll report us missing," Joanna said.

"Yeah, right. And the cops will come directly to Planet Doom. Don't you remember, Joanna? We pushed the board back into place. Nobody would see that it had been disturbed."

"You did that, Reggie. You idiot!" Joanna yelled. "That was really genius. If you hadn't done that, someone would see the opening. They would figure out we were in here."

"But you shouldn't have talked me into it in the first place. We wouldn't be in this mess at all," Reggie said. "None of this would be happening. You should have just kept your big mouth shut."

Joanna crumpled in a heap on the

ground. "Oh, Reggie," she sobbed. "Listen to us! We're at each other's throats. It's like *Survivor*. Turning on each other won't do us any good. We are trapped here!"

"Nothing is going to do us any good, Joanna. That man is a psycho. I have no doubts about him. He doesn't want us to get out of here alive. He probably came in here just after the fire. The dude appointed himself the protector of this park. He defends Eddie's reputation. You heard him say he was a big fan of that loser. That gives him a purpose in life. He hangs around here with his creepy disguises. He keeps this place alive. It should have been razed. These poor fools wander in. He gives them a few thrills. Then lets 'em die. I bet there are bodies buried all over this place!"

"Oh, gross," Joanna cried. "Do you really think this has happened to other people? Are there really dead bodies inside the park?" Her voice trembled.

"Sure," Reggie said. "Lots of people disappear. Kids our age, especially. One day they're here. And the next day they're gone. Everybody thinks they ran away. Maybe some did. But maybe not all of them. Maybe some of them ended up right here at Planet Doom. Remember Jimmy Wayne? He just vanished last spring. Maybe he wandered in here just like we did."

"Everybody said he went off to join a band," Joanna said.

"Maybe. Or maybe what's left of him is around here somewhere. Maybe we'll stumble over his bones—"

"Reggie!" Joanna cried. "Stop talking like that!"

"And Rami Singh. They said he got mixed up with a bad crowd. But maybe the truth is that he came to Planet Doom instead," Reggie said. "Maybe he fell into that weird man's trap too."

Chapter 8

We can't just give up!" Joanna said. "There must be a way we can get out of here. What are these walls made of? Maybe we could chip some holes. Make little footholds. Come on, Reggie, let's at least try!"

"It's no use," he said. "This looks like the end of the line, babe."

"Okay for you, Reggie. Go ahead and be a quitter if you want to!" Joanna snapped. She went to the wall. Her nail file made little dents in the surface. She felt encouraged. "Sweet, look! I chipped it a little. We can made places for our feet. Then we could just climb out!"

Reggie glared at Joanna. But what was there to lose? He joined her, chipping at the wall with his small penknife. After a few minutes, though, he gave up. "All we can do is make tiny holes. By the time we could carve out bigger ones, we'd be too exhausted to use them."

"Come on, help me!" Joanna cried. She stabbed her nail file into the wall again and again.

"We might as well just sit here and rest. Then we'll die of thirst or hunger," Reggie said. He leaned back and closed his eyes. "It's more peaceful this way."

Joanna continued to work. She knelt on the dirt and picked at the slippery walls. But before long she stopped. Even she had to admit that she was making almost no progress. And her knees were starting to hurt from kneeling on the hard ground.

Then she saw something. "Look, Reggie, there are tracks over there!" she cried.

"So what?" Reggie said with a tired groan.

"Some kind of little vehicle must have traveled down here. It must have come down the slide where we fell. Where did it go? It must have gone somewhere! Reggie, look! The tracks go over to this wall. The ride must have taken the people down the slope and—Reggie! There's a door here. It has to lead somewhere!" Joanna shouted.

Reggie moved quickly. He leaned hard on the white door. It blended exactly into the white walls. Eventually, it yielded. "A tunnel. It's a tunnel!"

"The little cars must have gone flying down the slope. Then they disappeared into the tunnel as a part of the ride. Come on, let's try to get out through it!"

"With our luck it probably leads right to the old psycho," Reggie said in disgust. But he went first, leading the way slowly. Since it was very dark, the two teens held hands so they wouldn't get separated. Along the way, they splashed through puddles of water.

"Keep moving, Reggie," Joanna said. "I bet this leads to a place at the fence!"

"Yeah, right! " Reggie said.

"Be positive! Hurry!" Joanna said. "Maybe the old man will look in the pit to check up on us. He'll see we're gone. Then he's sure to come after us."

"And he has those vicious dogs. They'll attack us," Reggie added.

The tunnel turned in a wide arc. Joanna could imagine the little cars on the tracks. The cars would turn wide. Riders would scream in delight.

"Hey, Joanna, do you hear that weird music?" Reggie asked.

"Yeah, it's really spooky. Like the music they play in slasher flicks just before something bad happens," Joanna said with a shudder.

"Oops!" Reggie grunted. He had bumped into a wall. But actually it was another door. Shoving it open, he saw a ramp leading upward. Joanna and Reggie followed the tracks until they came to a huge room. The first thing they noticed was that it had no roof. It had been burned off in the fire.

The two looked up. They could see the moon and the stars. The badly scorched walls around them revealed colorful paintings of some planet's stark environment. There were barren desert-like scenes with strange, twisted plants.

Joanna could see there had once been a roller coaster within this room. No doubt it was the final thrill of the ride that had begun with a slide down the slippery slope.

There was a faded sign. Reggie read it aloud. "*Welcome to Proxima Centauri, the nearest star to Earth. As you see, it is extremely dry and desolate …*" Reggie couldn't read the rest of the sign. The flames had burned the words away.

"Now how do we get out of this building?" Reggie asked Joanna. He was looking around frantically. "Okay, let's try that door over there."

But the door was jammed shut. They could see that the fire had melted the hardware.

"Oh no!" Joanna cried in a panicky voice. "What if there is no way out? What will we do? Will we have to go back to the pit?"

Reggie looked up. "I figure it's about a hundred feet up to the roof. Maybe we could crawl up to those burned rafters. But, oh man, if we fall from there …"

Chapter 9

The two continued to look around. Soon they found another door. To their relief, it opened. It was now after midnight. Overhead, the moon beamed like a giant searchlight. Just seeing the big white moon spilling its light was comforting.

Outside, Joanna and Reggie struggled to get their bearings. The skeleton-like hulks of burned buildings surrounded them. This end of the park had obviously gotten the worst of the fire.

"We've got to head for the closest part of the fence. That weirdo and his dogs could be anywhere. If he sees us, we're in big trouble," Reggie said.

Holding hands, they ran through the ruins. They searched for the fence. But they heard the barking of the man's dogs.

"The dogs smell us," Joanna yelled. "Oh, Reggie, they sound so close!"

"Hurry, babe!" Reggie yelled.

Just then, the dark shapes of the two dogs came roaring out of the darkness. Snarling and snapping, the big animals leaped over the debris.

"We'll never make it!" Reggie cried. He looked around desperately. They had reached a Ferris wheel just as the dogs caught up to them. The two hopped into a car. Joanna pulled the door shut. At the same moment a furious dog leaped at them. It howled in frustration.

Suddenly the lights of the Ferris wheel blinked on. The giant wheel began to move. How was that possible? Some of the cars were badly burned. The entire mechanism was damaged beyond repair. As it turned, the great wheel groaned. It sounded as if it were about to break at any moment.

The man then appeared. He shined his flashlight up at Reggie and Joanna. Their little car had almost reached the top now. Even in the dark, they saw that the cowboy's mask was gone. The man was old.

"Come down from there," the old man shouted. "The Ferris wheel is broken. The cars could drop at any moment. You must open the door of your car. Then climb down on the steel frame of the wheel."

"Yeah, sure! No way!" Reggie screamed in reply. "Maybe get crushed by moving parts. And then eaten by your dogs!"

The man rushed to the controls of the ride. When it had been working properly, the cars had always stayed upright as the great wheel turned. But now the wheel groaned. Some of the cars turned upside down. The broken and melted pulleys and gears clanged against one another. The engine kept struggling to turn the wheel. The skeleton frame of the ride was mangled. The whining of the stressed metal grew steadily louder.

Joanna and Reggie's car stalled on the very top of the wheel. The red, blue, and green lights on the towering ride made a lurid sight in the darkness. They flashed on and off.

"What if the car falls?" Joanna asked fearfully. She stared out at the twisted metal holding their car in place.

"Let's hope—" Reggie started to say. But then the Ferris wheel began turning again. The old man had gotten it started. Now their car was moving down. It was nearly within the grasp of the crazy old man! They could see him standing below. He held a crowbar in his hand as he waited for their car. The expression on his face was twisted and wild.

Without the smiling cowboy mask, they could see his real face. It was withered, lined, and scarred with bitterness. He waited for their car to come down. Then he started swinging the crowbar like a baseball bat.

Chapter 10

Then Joanna and Reggie saw something amazing. Fire trucks and police cars streamed into the park. Their sirens screamed. Dozens of startled neighbors had made calls when they saw the lights on the Ferris wheel. Something strange was going on behind the plywood fence!

The man and his dogs began to run. But they were soon caught. Out of concern for his pets' safety, the old man ordered the dogs to be docile. An officer from animal control took them off without harm. The police took charge of the man.

A firefighter helped Joanna and Reggie climb down from the broken ride.

"Thank God you came! We could have been killed," Joanna cried gratefully.

"Man, we really thought we were goners," Reggie said.

"What were you kids doing here anyway?" a police officer asked. "Didn't you see the signs? There is no trespassing! This is a horribly dangerous place."

"We were stupid," Reggie said. "We thought it would be okay to just take a look behind the fence."

"Yes," Joanna said. "It turned out that was not a smart idea."

The couple described all that had happened. A police officer drove them home.

♦ • ♦

It wasn't until the following day that they made a sad discovery.

Both teenagers were called down to the police station. Each had to give further information about their ordeal. A police officer named Tessa Jones told them who was behind their ordeal. "The man who terrorized you is Ross Scott," she said. "He is the father of Eddie Scott, the baseball player who paid for the amusement park."

"His father?" Reggie gasped. "I thought he was a homeless man who had nowhere else to go. Wow! Eddie Scott's dad! I bet Eddie will be upset when he finds out what his old man has been up to."

"That's why he was so upset when you called Eddie a loser," Joanna said. "And that's why he wanted to keep the place going. He wanted to honor his son. He was trying to take care of his son's creation."

"Poor old guy," Reggie said. He felt a wave of sympathy for the man who had caused them so much misery. "I guess he was really crushed when his son got kicked out of baseball. Especially after everybody in the neighborhood had such high hopes."

"Yeah," Joanna said. "Eddie spent all his

money on Planet Doom. When it burned, he didn't have that or his career either."

"Where's Eddie now?" Reggie asked. "He's got to come down here. Take care of his old man. He needs to get the old guy into a good hospital. I am sure he can get help there."

"When Eddie got dropped from the majors, he tried a lot of different jobs. He even worked as a handyman for a while. But nothing worked out for him. He had blown all his money on the amusement park. Pretty soon he was living on the street," Officer Jones said. "From time to time, we'd pick him up. Get him cleaned up. Eddie was drinking pretty heavily by then. He was really a sad case."

"Oh no," Reggie said. "I didn't know. Nobody did. And now this."

"Eddie is feeling no pain now," Officer Jones said. "On one of those really cold nights we had last January, he slept under some newspapers in an alley. Somebody noticed him. The paramedics were called. But by that time he wasn't sleeping anymore. He had died of exposure. He was only twenty-five years old. We took up a collection to bury him."

Joanna looked at Reggie. Tears welled up in her eyes. Then she turned to Officer Jones. "How could such a thing happen? How could something so awful happen to a guy who had it all?" she asked.

"I guess he never got his skills back after the injury," Officer Jones said. "My husband and I used to go to the games. At the end Eddie brought the team down. People would yell at him. They threw things at him. It just wore him down. Just imagine doing your job as best you can. Then screaming fans are yelling terrible things at you. They are telling you that you aren't good anymore.

Imagine a stadium full of people who hate your guts. And why? Just because you've disappointed them."

Joanna slipped her hand into Reggie's. "I hope when they build over Planet Doom, they leave something of Eddie's in place. Maybe the little museum or something. Everybody should remember that he tried to do something nice for the people in his old neighborhood," she said.

Reggie nodded. He stared over at the Ferris wheel. It was dark now. But it loomed over the neighborhood. "Maybe we could get a little online petition going," he said. "I can text all my friends. Maybe there could at least be a little plaque in the new mall. Something that says Eddie Scott was a good-hearted guy."

Joanna gave Reggie a hug. "Good idea. I'll do something too," she said.

♦ • ♦

Eddie's dad was recovering in a hospital.

No charges had been filed against him. He was unfit to stand trial. Some people in the country adopted his dogs. They had room to run.

Just about everybody in the old neighborhood signed the petition. People wanted Eddie to finally be recognized.

The heavy equipment moved in. Planet Doom was soon razed. All that was left was dirt and sad memories.

A few years later, there was a ribbon-cutting ceremony. A big bronze plaque was embedded in the entrance to the brand new mall. The mall was named Eddie Scott Plaza.

Comprehension Questions

Recall

1. Why did a plywood fence surround the amusement park?

2. Why had Planet Doom been built in a rundown neighborhood?

3. Who offered Reggie and Joanna a lifetime pass to Planet Doom? What would they have to do to get it?

Analyzing Characters

1. Which character in the story could be described as unstable? Explain your thinking.

2. Which character tried harder to get out of the pit? Give an example.

Vocabulary

1. Reggie and Joanna were desperate to leave. What does *desperate* mean?

2. The cowboy's dogs were named Homerun and Shutout. In baseball, what does *shutout* mean?

3. The cowboy terrorized Reggie and Joanna. What does *terrorize* mean?

Cause and Effect

1. What caused Reggie to become so uncomfortable and afraid when he took the Mars ride?

2. What did the cowboy do that caused Reggie to fall to the ground?